FRIENDSHIP (

Pibbin
the
Small

A Tale of Friendship Bog

Gloria Repp

illustrated by Tim Davis

Library of Congress Catalog Number
2011916795

ISBN-13: 978-1466313781
ISBN-10: 1466313781

Printed in the United States of America

Contents

Chapter 1

Rumble Road

Ma Chipmunk had tears in her eyes. "It's Cheeco. His cough is so bad!"

Pibbin hopped closer to the little chipmunk. Sleeping? Not frisking around? Not getting into trouble? The kid must be really sick.

"Please?" Ma Chipmunk said. "Please ask Sheera what I should give him?"

"I've been trying to find her," Pibbin said. His friend would know the best thing for a cough, but where had that turtle gone?

1

He hopped down to Friendship Bog.

Sheera wouldn't be sitting on the lily pads —she was too big. She liked to nap by the water or catch spiders in the bushes. Sometimes she sat on Woodpecker Log to enjoy the sun.

Not there. Not anywhere.

What about Sheera's home pool? It was close by, a handy place for visitors. Everyone came to ask her advice when they were sick.

No, not there either.

Maybe she'd gone into the pine woods to dig for beetles.

He hopped across the pine needles and over the sandy ground, but he couldn't find even a claw mark.

She had to be here, somewhere! He climbed onto a log to look around.

Ahead of him was Rumble Road.

He didn't like to go anywhere near the road, but Carpenter Frog stood there, and so did Gaffer the Gray Treefrog.

A squirrel stood there too, and three mice, and a rabbit with her children.

What had happened? Better find out.

He jumped down from the log, and Gaffer came to meet him. "Just a minute, Pib," he said. "I have some bad news."

The old treefrog's face wrinkled up, as if he were sad. "It's Sheera."

"What? What about her?"

"I'm sorry, Pib."

"No, not Sheera," Pibbin said. "There's a mistake. I'm sure there's a mistake."

Something inside him began to hurt, and he had to talk about her.

"She saved my life, did you know?" he said. "I was just learning to hop, and one day a hawk came after me, and I dived for cover. I ended up under her shell. She didn't mind a bit."

"Yes," Gaffer said. "I remember. She's been a good friend to you. And to all of us."

"So, where is she? What's the matter?"

Gaffer turned toward the road. "Come and see."

Pibbin hopped along beside him until they reached the edge of the road. He stopped.

Sheera was lying out there in the sand.

"A truck," the squirrel said. "Going fast."

"Too many trucks," the mouse said. Her voice squeaked. "My sister! That's how she got run over."

"Hear that?" the rabbit said to her children. "Keep away from the road!"

Gaffer hopped into the middle of Rumble Road. He bent close to look at Sheera, and she lifted her head.

"She's alive," he said. "Let's get her away from here."

Carpenter brought his wagon to carry Sheera back to her pool, and everyone helped.

Finally they slid her off the wagon and stood around to watch. One of her legs was bleeding. She had pulled her head back into her shell.

Gaffer sighed. "I wish we had a doctor in Friendship Bog."

The squirrel picked an armful of ferns and piled them onto Sheera. "There. Ferns will help."

"No, that's silly," the mouse said. "Give her worm juice. But it has to be fresh."

"No, we need to wake her up first," the rabbit said. "Pour cold water on her shell."

After a long time, they stopped talking and went away.

Pibbin watched them leave. Ferns? Worm juice? Cold water?

Sheera was the one who knew the best way to fix a bleeding leg.

What could he do?

Chapter 2
Silver Sea

Pibbin crept close to his friend.

"Wonk?" he said, very low.

Sheera poked her head out a little way.

"Do you want some water?" he asked.

"Yes."

He got her a drink from the pool. "I'll be here if you need anything."

She shut her eyes and didn't answer.

He waited.

The sun set, and the bushes grew dark, and a cool breeze blew up from the bog. He sat close beside her to wait and watch.

He listened for the peeper frogs. They always had something to say, but now they were quiet. Were they worried about Sheera too?

After a while he caught four redbugs and ate them. He took one to Sheera, but she didn't seem to wake up when he talked to her.

A shadow, darker than night, flew over the pool. An owl. Had it seen him? He jumped into a bush where he'd be safe and settled down to wait some more.

She did not move. All through the long hours of the night, she did not move.

In the morning, Sheera poked her head out of her shell. She stretched out her three good legs. She tried to pull herself down to the water, but all she could do was scratch at the mud.

He took her another drink. He picked a dangleberry for her, and she ate it.

Her leg was still bleeding a little, so he slid a bit of moss under it for a pillow.

He put a gentle hand on her shell. Such a beautiful brown and yellow shell! Now it had a crack in it.

When he was just a froglet, he'd wanted to grow a shell like hers. But then she'd told him that shells were for turtles, not frogs, and he'd been unhappy for days.

"Sheera," he said. "What do you need?"

Her golden eyes looked dull. "Sweetberry leaves."

"I'll get some!"

"Not around here. All gone."

He climbed into the biggest bush by the pool. "Here's some dangleberry leaves," he said. "Nice and green. I can make a wrap for your leg, like you did for Granny Mouse. "

"Need Sweetberry." Sheera's eyes began to close, but she said, "I have a friend who grows it. She's a doctor."

"Where's your friend live?"

"Silver Sea." Her voice faded as she pulled her head back into the shell.

Pibbin stayed in the dangleberry bush and watched her sleep.

Sheera had told him stories about Silver Sea. "It has such wonderful waves," she said. "A hundred times bigger than you've ever seen."

Sometimes the waves looked blue and gold. Sometimes they looked green and gray.

All day long, they lapped and splashed and foamed on the shore. After dark, they gleamed with a cool, silver light.

Every time she talked about Silver Sea, he wanted to go and look at those waves.

Carpenter hopped through the bushes. "How's she doing?" he asked.

"I'm not sure," Pibbin said. "She ate a little bit."

"Good, good!" Carpenter hopped closer. "How's the leg? Can she bend it?"

10

"I don't think so," Pibbin said.

"How about her foot?"

"It doesn't seem to bend right."

Carpenter frowned. "Not so good. She's gotta have all four of those legs working."

He put a hand on his tool belt. "We might have to give her a new leg."

"How?"

"I can do it," Carpenter said.

"Really?"

"I'll tell ya a true story," Carpenter said. "I knew an old turtle. A rat chewed on his leg, one winter when he was sound asleep. A bad bite. The leg got worse, then it dried up, and then it fell off. I fixed him up with a new one. Made it out of wood."

Pibbin looked down at his own legs. "Did the new leg bend?"

"Nope."

Pibbin stretched out his leg. It bent nicely in two places. What if it were just a stick?

12

He shook his head. "I want Sheera to keep her leg. It's real."

Carpenter shrugged and turned to leave.

"Wait!" Pibbin said. "Do you know how to get to Silver Sea?"

"Nope, sure don't. But they say it's a long trip." He frowned at Pibbin. "A long, long trip. Don't you try it."

After he'd gone, Sheera whispered a name, and Pibbin bent low to hear.

"Gaffer. He knows," she said.

Pibbin took another look at Sheera's leg and hurried off to Gaffer's tree house.

He found the old gray treefrog napping on his deck.

"Hello, hello," Gaffer said. "You have a question on your face."

"It's Sheera's leg! She's not getting any better," Pibbin said. "What can we do?"

Gaffer leaned forward in his rocking chair. "Sweetberry leaves are best," he said.

He frowned. "But all of a sudden, it's hard to find Sweetberry. I don't understand why."

"Maybe there's some growing down at Silver Sea." Pibbin gazed into the pine trees. "Maybe someone could go and get it."

"Yes," Gaffer said. He gazed into the pine trees too.

"She told me there's a doctor at Silver Sea."

"Yes," Gaffer said.

"Do you know the way to Silver Sea?"

"Yes. Yes, I do."

The old treefrog rocked back and forth, and a breeze rattled the pine branches, and down by the bog, the peeper frogs sang.

"It's a long, long trip," Pibbin said. "I guess I'm too small to go that far."

Gaffer kept rocking. "No one is too small to be brave," he said. "How big is your heart? That's what counts."

Pibbin wanted to creep away under a bush. He felt as small as an ant, and his heart felt smaller than a grain of sand. Maybe it was too small to be brave.

"There's a bus," Gaffer said. "It's called the Shore Express. I know the driver—Fridd. He's a little old toad with a scar on his chin and big blue boots. He'd help you."

Pibbin thought about the bus and the nice little old toad. Maybe he could be brave enough for that.

"But," Gaffer said, "what you really need is a pal."

Chapter 3

Quick and Smart

Pibbin took his time as he hopped back toward Sheera's pool.

Gaffer had said two important things: *Get the doctor's name.* And, *Find yourself a pal who is quick and smart.*

He stopped beside a tall pine stump. How about a snack? He ate a spider and two brown beetles and four black ants, but something inside him still felt empty. Did he really want to go all the way to Silver Sea?

A tapping sound came from the other side of the stump. Carpenter must be building something for the mice who lived there.

Pibbin hopped around to the back of the stump. Carpenter was smart, and he could hammer fast. Maybe he'd make a good pal.

The old brown frog was working halfway up the stump.

"How's it going?" Pibbin asked.

"Not bad, not bad at all. I like building decks." Carpenter leaned down. "Hand me that stick, would you, kiddo?"

Pibbin picked up the long piece of wood. He stood on his tiptoes but couldn't lift it high enough for Carpenter to reach.

He started to climb up with it, and the stick slipped to the ground.

"Okay, okay, I might have known," Carpenter said. "You're still kinda small, aren't you?"

He jumped down to get the stick. "Did you talk to Old Gaff about Silver Sea?"

"Yes," Pibbin said.

This would be a good time to ask him about being a pal.

Pibbin opened his mouth, but Carpenter was looking stern.

"I hope he told you to forget about taking that trip," Carpenter said.

He picked up his hammer. "You'll never make it there and back. Wait a while, kiddo."

Pibbin wanted to say, *What about Sheera?* but he felt as if he'd choked on a beetle.

Slowly he hopped away. He should go and see how she was doing. Maybe she was awake now. Maybe her leg had stopped bleeding. And maybe no one would have to go to Silver Sea.

Sheera seemed to be asleep. Ma Chipmunk was bending over her, and Cheeco was running circles around the two of them.

"Cheeco looks better," Pibbin said.

But the last thing Sheera needed was this kid zooming up and down.

Ma Chipmunk smiled. "I remembered the red-root juice that Sheera uses. It really helped."

Cheeco bounced up to Pibbin. "Look at me! I'm getting bigger every day!"

He tapped Pibbin's arm and almost knocked him over. "You're IT. Catch me if you can!"

He darted away, and Ma Chipmunk turned back to talk about Sheera.

"I don't know." Her plump little face looked worried. "I just don't know what to do about that leg. I think it should have stopped bleeding by now."

Cheeco bounced back. "Ha! Ha! She gonna get a stick for a leg? Is she? Is she? I wanna watch!"

Pibbin dragged himself up into a bush. First, get away from the kid. Then, think.

"Sheera needs Sweetberry leaves," he said.

He curled his toes around the branch— curled them tight. Finally he said, "I'm going to go and get some."

"Oh! Do be careful!" Ma Chipmunk said. "I hope she feels better soon. Cheeco, stop making all that noise and come with me."

After they had gone, Sheera poked her head out and looked at him. "Did you talk to Gaffer?"

Pibbin jumped down from the bush. "Yes," he said. "What's the name of your friend?"

"Doctor Diggitt." Sheera's eyes seemed to grow brighter. "She might like a present. Take her my hoop."

"Okay." Pibbin pushed the leaves off a hollow log where she kept the hoop and pulled it out. It was too big for his backpack, so he tied it onto the outside.

What next? Find someone quick and smart. But where?

He hopped along the edge of the pool. Peeper frogs sang everywhere, telling the news. Would they know of a good pal?

He could still hear the tapping of Carpenter's hammer. If only Carpenter would come!

"Hey there!" Bug-Master said. He stretched out his long, sticky tongue and caught three flies: Zap! Zap! Zap! "What's your hurry?"

"I'm going down to Silver Sea." Pibbin hopped closer to the big treefrog. "I'm looking for a pal who's quick, like you."

"Not today." Bug-Master had a ringing voice. "Aren't you afraid to take a trip like that? A snake might get you."

He snapped up a moth. "Or Old Boomer. He likes the taste of little frogs, you know."

Bug-Master turned and was gone before Pibbin could blink, but his voice rang through the bushes. "Be careful, small Pibbin. It's a long way to the sea."

"Sea, sea, sea!" called the peepers.

They sounded close by, and Pibbin looked around to find them. Three of the tiny frogs grinned at him from a branch. They were the smallest of his friends, and they seemed to know he was scared.

"Wonk!" Pibbin said to them. "That's where I'm going. No matter what."

The peepers grinned in reply, and then a frog's bright song floated across the pool: *"Cree-eeee-eek. Cree-eeee-eek."*

He hopped toward it. Corey! He wasn't very big, but he'd be smart and quick. Sure. He'd be just right for a pal.

Chapter 4
Scared?

The little striped frog finished his song and smiled. "Hi, Pib! What's new?"

"I'm going down to Silver Sea," Pibbin said.

"Where's that? At the shore? How come you're going?"

"I need to get some special leaves for Sheera."

"For her leg? Does it look bad? Does she want a nurse?"

"I don't know," Pibbin said.

Corey always asked more questions than anyone could answer.

Pibbin looked at his friend. "I need someone to go with me."

Corey had stopped smiling. "I'm sorry about Sheera," he said. "She's the nicest turtle I ever met. But I just . . . can't . . . go. We'd have to cross Rumble Road, wouldn't we?"

"I guess so."

"And what if we ran into a coon? Or a fox? Or those Black Snapping Crabs?" Corey shook his head. "I'd be so scared! You don't need someone like me."

Too bad! Corey was the smartest frog he'd ever met.

Corey looked down at his toes. "I wish I could help you," he whispered.

Pibbin tried to think of something to say, and Corey glanced up. "Wait! I don't want you to get lost."

Corey hopped away and soon came back with a piece of paper. "You need a map."

He spread it out on the pine needles. "See? Here's Friendship Bog, and that dot is Sheera's pool. The little tree mark is Gaffer's tree house. And here's Rumble Road."

Rumble Road looked like a thin white snake, curving down the map.

Corey said, "After you cross Rumble Road, you'll have to go through—oh, my!—Bullfrog Bog." He shivered. "And look! Down here is Wild Bog. Stay away from that place. I hear it's full of Black Snapping Crabs."

Pibbin didn't want to think about bullfrogs or snapping crabs. "Gaffer said to take the Shore Express."

"Excellent!" Corey said. "You can ride the Express all the way south to the shore, and you'll be fine."

Pibbin nodded, but he didn't feel fine.

"Here." Corey folded up the map and handed it to him. "It's got a cover to keep it dry, and it might be useful."

Corey's dark eyes still looked unhappy. He said, "I'm a nurse, you know. I'll take care of Sheera while you're gone."

"Thank you," Pibbin said, and he put the map into his backpack. "It's always good to have a map."

"Map, map, map!" called the peepers.

"Map?" A leopard frog poked his head out of the grass. "For your trip? I heard about that, Pib. Need someone to go with you?"

"Wonk!" Pibbin began to smile.

Leeper was the best jumper in Friendship Bog. He'd be a great pal.

Right away, Leeper sat down with the map. He asked questions and made plans.

"Ready?" he said at last. "Let's get going. First, we cross Rumble Road."

Pibbin didn't say anything.

He followed Leeper to the road and slowly started across it. He dug his toes into the sand. His legs began to shake.

This road looked too wide, like a big river of sand. It felt too dry, enough to make his head ache. And what if another fast truck came along?

Leeper didn't seem to mind it. "Look and listen," he said. "Then go quick as you can."

He scrambled through the hills of soft sand and hopped over the ruts, and Pibbin hurried after him.

More trees and bushes grew on the other side, like they did in his own pine woods. This might not be such a bad trip, after all.

By evening, they had reached Bullfrog Bog.

"Rumm . . . rumm . . . ru-u-u-um," said a big booming voice.

"Oh-oh," Leeper said, and Pibbin began to worry. Leeper looked toward the top of the bog. "But it sounds like he's hunting up there."

"Good!" Pibbin said. If Boomer the Giant Bullfrog was that far away, they'd be safe.

He jumped into the water with a *wonk* of joy. Wet! Cool! Hurrah!

But what was this? Long thin legs stepping close. A sharp beak stabbing down—

He jerked away. Swim fast! Dive deep!

He slid into the mud at the bottom of the bog and stayed there, shaking.

Almost got him. If only his legs were longer and stronger!

He watched the feet that belonged to the legs, and after a while, they walked off.

Where had Leeper gone? There he was, under a floating bush.

30

Pibbin swam over to join him, and Leeper grinned. "Good for you, pal. Those birds are fast, but you were faster. Let's keep moving."

It took them the whole night to travel down Bullfrog Bog.

Sometimes they swam. Sometimes they stopped to climb over dead trees, or hop across a muddy patch, or crawl through tall grass.

Pibbin didn't mind. Every minute, they were getting farther away from Boomer and closer to Silver Sea.

Leeper had a tricky dive that zigged and zagged. "I wish I could do that," Pibbin said.

"Use what you've got," Leeper said. "I can't climb trees."

He grinned. "Tomorrow we'll get to the swamp at the bottom of the bog. It's full of trees."

"Good!" Pibbin said. "Maybe we'll find some Sweetberry leaves there."

When morning came, they were both tired, so they took a rest beside the bog.

In the swamp, the trees looked like long, gray poles. No leaves. A few trees stood tall, but most of them leaned across each other with vines hanging almost to the ground.

Pibbin liked the quiet trees, and the vines, and the puddles of water. But some snakes liked water too, didn't they?

A snake might get you, Bug-Master had said.

He leaped onto a fallen tree, away from the water, and caught some flying bugs for lunch.

From there he hopped onto a leaning tree and used it as a bridge to a taller tree. He crawled out along one of its smooth gray branches and sat under a vine to watch for snakes. Leeper stayed on a log below, eating caterpillars.

A sweet, light voice came from the branch above him. "Hello!"

Pibbin stared up into the face of a snake.

Jump! But his legs felt like wood, and he couldn't even wiggle his toes.

Chapter 5

Leaps and Kicks

Pibbin kept his eyes on the snake. Any minute now, his legs might work again, and he'd jump.

Why was this snake smiling? Did they always smile, just before they attacked?

"Oh, please!" the snake said. "Please don't go away." It slid toward him, green and slender as the vine.

Now he could wiggle his toes. He jumped down to the next branch.

"Please!" the green snake said again. "I'm a friend of Sheera's, and I heard about your trip. You must be Pibbin."

Was it a trick? But this snake wasn't big enough to eat a frog, not even a small treefrog like him. Okay, he'd listen.

"I'm Miss Green." The snake glided closer. "I just want to say that I'm glad you're doing this. It won't be easy."

"I have a pal," Pibbin said, and he took her down to talk to Leeper.

She smiled at them. "Tell me, is there any way I can help you?"

"We've got a map," Leeper said. "But now we have to find the Shore Express."

"I've seen it go by." Miss Green dipped her head. "It stops at a marker stone on the other side of the swamp."

"What's the best way to get there?" Leeper asked.

"After a while you'll come to a stream," she said. "You can follow it out of the swamp."

"Sounds like a plan," he said. "Thanks."

That night they found the stream, and it felt good to swim in the cool, dark water. If only they could float all the way to the shore!

By early morning, the stream had become a wide pond. "I'm guessing the beavers did this," Leeper said.

Sure enough, at the far end of the pond, they found a dam made of sticks and branches.

They climbed up onto the dam and looked across it.

All Pibbin could see was grass and puddles of water.

Where were they?

"Let's take a look at that map," Leeper said.

Pibbin unfolded it. Here was Bullfrog Bog, with the swamp at the bottom of it.

A wiggly line came out of the swamp. That must be the stream they had followed.

The map didn't show the dam or the grass, but he found an X that must be the marker stone for the Shore Express.

"We're going the right way," Leeper said. "We just have to keep going."

They hopped through the grass for a long time, and Leeper didn't seem to get tired.

Pibbin said, "I wish I had strong legs like yours."

"Use what you've got," Leeper said. He showed Pibbin his high-flying leaps and kicks.

Pibbin tried jumping over clumps of grass, higher and higher, until his legs began to wobble.

At last they came to a large, flat stone, and Leeper hopped onto it with a grin. "Our bus stop. We did it!"

Pibbin took off his pack and set it in the sun so the hoop would dry.

"Pretty," Leeper said. "It's a great present."

Pibbin nodded. Sheera's hoop glittered in the sunlight, and its red jewels glowed like tiny bits of fire.

The doctor would like it, but they still had a long way to go. How was Sheera feeling today?

They sat and waited. The sun rose high over their heads, and still they waited.

They took a nap and waited some more.

Pibbin jumped up to try out his new leaps and kicks. "Where's that bus?" He kicked his highest kick. "Maybe I'll climb a tree and take a look."

At first, all he could see was hundreds of pine trees and a narrow white road.

But what was this? Something that looked like a house on wheels was rushing along the road.

"Here it comes!" he called.

The bus rolled toward them, faster and faster.

Close up, the bus looked even more like a house—a dusty house. It had branches for walls, one tiny window, and a wooden door.

The driver was a brown spotted toad, but he didn't look very old.

Pibbin climbed down the tree as fast as he could.

The bus stopped beside the marker stone, and the driver jumped down from his seat. He was young and plump, and he wore tall black boots with yellow ties.

"Where's Fridd?" Pibbin asked.

"My uncle's sick," the toad said. "I'm driving today."

He opened the door of the bus and helped an old chipmunk step down onto the stone.

"Such a trip!" she said. "My bones are still rattling. Why do you have to drive so fast?"

The toad didn't answer, and she leaned on her cane as she limped across the stone. She stopped in front of Sheera's hoop.

"Oh, my! What a lovely thing."

"It's a present," Pibbin said. "For a doctor who lives down at Silver Sea. A woodchuck."

"That would be Doctor Diggitt. I've known her for years. But she has moved."

The chipmunk stopped talking and put a paw to her head. "Oh, my, my! I don't feel well. Not at all."

Leeper reached out his hand, and she held onto him. "Thank you. Such a fine, strong frog!"

"Do you know where the doctor lives now?" Leeper asked.

"Wild Bog. She's got a nice garden."

"Does the bus go there?" Pibbin asked.

"I don't think so," she said. "But I can tell you the way."

The toad stepped close. "Wait a minute!" He looked at Pibbin. "Why not have some fun first? I can give you a fast ride to Silver Sea."

He smiled. "You're so small, you don't need to pay."

The toad puffed out his chest. "And then I'll show you a shortcut to Wild Bog. I know all the shortcuts around here."

Pibbin thought about those wonderful gleaming waves. Why not?

He picked up his backpack and slowly put it on. Why not take a quick look at Silver Sea? Leeper would like the waves too.

But . . . Sheera was waiting.

"No," he said. "I don't think so."

"Sure! You'll have a fun time!" The toad's thick arm shot out toward Pibbin, lifted him up, and pushed him into the bus.

The door slammed shut.

The driver yelled something, and the bus started with a jerk.

Chapter 6

A Cage on Wheels

Pibbin crouched low. He heard the driver's boots stomping on the pedals. He felt the bus going faster and faster. It bumped over sticks and splashed through puddles like a fox with bees in his ears.

The driver must be crazy! Why had he done this?

Pibbin's pack bounced against his back, and he remembered Sheera's hoop. Did that toad want it for himself?

Get rid of it, quick!

The window had a clear covering nailed across it. The inside walls were made of boards nailed together.

He could see the toad's head through a window slit in the front. Stay away from there.

He looked at the back of the bus. Something smelled sweet, but all he could see was boxes.

Every time the bus bumped, the boxes bounced. Every time the boxes bounced, they banged against the back wall of the bus.

He crawled toward them.

Maybe he could hide the hoop in a box.

The next time the boxes bounced, a crack showed between the boards, and he thought of a better plan.

Watch the crack. What would happen if he pushed against it?

Good! It opened a little bit more.

He untied the hoop and pushed against the crack again.

Bump! The boxes banged hard against the wall. The crack opened wide. He slipped the hoop through, and it dropped out of sight.

He'd come back and pick it up later, but now he had to escape.

Window? Tight.

Door? Locked.

This was a cage on wheels.

He looked up at the roof. It was made of narrow boards that wiggled and jiggled and banged with every bump. But it was a long way over his head.

Use what you've got.

The sticky pads on his toes were good for climbing trees. Why not climb the walls of this cage? Try it!

He started climbing and soon found that the flat boards were more slippery than tree bark.

Keep going. Halfway up.

The driver glanced back through the window slit. "Hey, you! Get down from there."

Up higher. Quick! All the way to the roof.

He kicked at a loose board. He kicked and kicked until it moved, then he pulled himself up and out.

He jumped.

It felt more like a dive than a jump. Ouch! He'd landed in a thorn bush. But he was free, and the driver hadn't stopped.

He crawled out of the bush and began hopping back to look for the hoop.

A voice called, "Hey, pal!" Leeper was hurrying down the road toward him.

"Great escape!" Leeper said. "I found the hoop where you dropped it, and the chipmunk told me how to get to Wild Bog. We're all set."

"Let's hurry," Pibbin said, but he couldn't hop very fast.

"Let's be smart," Leeper said. "We're both hungry, and you need a rest. We can go faster at night, anyway. Let's make a plan."

After a good long nap, they set off again.

They had to cross a wide sandy road that Leeper thought might be part of Rumble Road. Tonight, it lay quiet under the stars.

Pine woods stood thick and dark on the other side, and Pibbin headed into them. Trees were safer, even if there wasn't a path.

Leeper soon stopped. "She told me to cross the road," he said. "Then take any path that goes to the west. I guess that would be a path that goes toward the setting sun."

He glanced at the trees above them. "But where? The sun has already set. Oh, I know!" He turned. "We have to go back to the road."

"Why?" Pibbin said.

Leeper had already reached the road. He stopped in the middle to look up at the sky. "Stars," he said. "The North star. There it is —come and see."

Pibbin hopped out to stand beside him and Leeper pointed into the sky over their heads.

"See where the stars make a little box, and three stars come out of it, like a long tail?"

"Where?" Pibbin said. "Okay, yes."

"The last of those three is the North star. It shows us which way is north."

"But she said to take a path going west."

"Right. And west is always this way from north." Leeper hopped toward the trees they had just come from.

"Let's see if we can find a path," he called back. "I'll go up the road, and you go down it."

He started off. "It shouldn't be too far."

"Here," Pibbin said, looking at a faint path through the bushes. "How's this one?"

"Goes west. It'll do," Leeper said. "Now we can make good time."

They reached Wild Bog early the next morning. The sun felt warm on Pibbin's back, but mist still hung above the water.

"Wow!" Leeper said. "I didn't know it was this big. I've got uncles living here, somewhere."

Pibbin gazed across the bog.

Floating bushes made humps in the mist. What about the Black Snapping Crabs? Were they hiding out there under those bushes?

He turned away. "We have to find the doctor," he said. "What do woodchucks eat?"

"Green stuff, I think." Leeper started off along the shore of the bog. "The chipmunk said to turn north when we got here. Let's look for a field."

They hopped under bushes and past stumps, and over moss and pine needles and dried leaves. Finally, Leeper said, "We've come a long way, and who knows what we'll run into next. How about a nap?"

"Good idea!"

Pibbin didn't want to stay near the bog, so they hopped toward the trees, found a thick bush, and slept beneath it.

The hunting cry of a red-tailed hawk jerked him awake.

He slid deep into the dried leaves under the bush, and Leeper did the same.

After a long while, he heard mouse feet pattering by and knew that the hawk had gone.

They set off again, and soon Pibbin said, "It seems like we're climbing a little hill. Look on the other side of those bushes. Do you think it might be an open space?"

"I hope so," Leeper said. "I sure am ready to find that doctor."

They crawled through bushes with vines that looped over and under and every which way.

The thorns on the vines snatched at Leeper's hat and Pibbin's backpack. He ducked low to keep the hoop from getting scratched.

At last they came to a field of grass and wild flowers. "Here's a path," Leeper said. "I wonder who made it."

Pibbin wondered too. "It's too small for a deer path, and too big for a mouse path."

At least it couldn't be a snapping-crab path, he told himself. Crabs would stay in the water. Wouldn't they?

The path climbed up a small grassy hill and curved around a clump of bushes. Pibbin stopped to listen.

Snarr . . . snarggle . . . k-k-k.

Snarr . . . snarggle . . . k-k-k.

"What's that?" he asked, and Leeper shrugged.

Someone snoring? He crept through the bushes to see.

Chapter 7

Sweetberry Somewhere

An animal—large and brown—lay sleeping in the grass.

Snarr . . . snarggle . . . k-k-k.

It had round ears, so it wasn't a fox. It had a big thick body, so it wasn't a weasel. It had a bushy brown tail, so it wasn't a super-sized rabbit.

"Woodchuck?" Pibbin whispered.

"Guess so," Leeper said. "Maybe it's the doctor."

The snoring stopped.

"What? What?" the woodchuck mumbled. "Come back later. Unless you're bleeding."

Snarggle . . . snarr . . . snarr . . .

This had to be the doctor. Pibbin watched her sleep. He didn't want to wake her up, but too many days had passed since they'd left Sheera.

He took three small hops forward. "Um, excuse me?"

Snarr . . . snarr . . .

"Doctor? My friend Sheera—"

The woodchuck rolled onto her side. She yawned, showing two long, sharp teeth.

Pibbin jumped back.

The doctor blinked. "Who? Sheera? My friend at Silver Sea?"

"Yes, but she's living at Friendship Bog now," Pibbin said. "She's my friend too. We came to see you because her leg is hurt."

The doctor sat up. "How bad?"

"Bleeding. And stiff. And her foot doesn't work right."

"Hmmm," the doctor said. "A truck?"

"Yes."

"I knew it. They shouldn't let those trucks on our roads." The doctor looked more awake. "Not at all! Close the roads, I say!"

She leaned over and snapped off a mouthful of grass. "How about her shell? Cracked?"

"Just one little crack," Pibbin said. "But her leg! Will it fall off? Will she have to get a wooden one?"

"Fizzle! How foolish! Just wrap that leg in Sweetberry leaves, and after a while she'll be good as new."

The doctor leaned back and closed her eyes. "Such a nice warm day."

"Wait!" Pibbin pulled off his backpack. "Sheera sent you a present."

He untied the hoop and held it out. The three red jewels gleamed, bright as a smile.

The doctor sat up again. "I remember that. I was there when Sheera found it," she said quietly.

"We were walking in the sand at Silver Sea. Prettiest thing, isn't it? But she doesn't have to give me her hoop."

"She wants to," Pibbin said. "Please, she needs some Sweetberry leaves."

"I think I have a few left." Doctor Diggitt picked up the hoop, and it looked small in her thick brown claws. "Let's go see."

She led them down the other side of the hill to her burrow. Her door had a note pinned to it: **OUT for NAP.**

She swung the door open and pinned the hoop onto the inside. "There! To remind me of my beautiful friend. Be right back."

Pibbin sat down to wait, and Leeper did too.

The doctor seemed to be gone for hours. Was she taking another nap?

He thought about Sheera. He thought about snapping crabs and hungry snakes and crazy toad-drivers. He thought about the long trip back to Friendship Bog.

Doctor Diggitt finally waddled out of her burrow. "Couldn't find any." She frowned. "I probably used the last ones for that possum's back. Another truck case."

She must have seen the look on Pibbin's face, because she said, "Maybe we can pick some fresh leaves. I just hope they're ripe."

She led them along a path that curved down toward the bog, and Pibbin remembered the snapping crabs. Maybe they didn't live in this part of the bog, but he had to ask.

"Do you have much trouble around here with Black Snapping Crabs?"

The woodchuck looked back at him. "Fizzle! How foolish! They died out years ago."

Pibbin hopped more quickly, and the day seemed brighter. No more snapping crabs! Corey would be glad to know it.

The doctor looked back at him again. "Did Sheera tell you about my garden?"

"No," Pibbin said. "She was too sick."

By now, she might be even sicker. Was Corey getting her something to eat?

"Here we are," Doctor Diggitt said with a smile. "I had to put a fence around it because of the deer. They know what's good."

Pibbin gazed at the rows of plants. Which ones were Sweetberry?

The doctor picked a leaf and held it out to them. "Doesn't this smell like apples? It's good for burns."

She pointed to a low, prickly bush. "And this is red-root. I use it for coughs."

So did Sheera.

"Here's tansy," the doctor said. "I knew an old rabbit . . ."

Pibbin tried to listen to her story about the rabbit who had something wrong with his head.

Was she going to talk all day? Sheera must be wondering what had happened to them.

He did two high hops, then a sideways kick, so he wouldn't forget how.

The woodchuck bent to pick a leaf from another plant, and Pibbin said, "Please, Doctor Diggitt, where's the Sweetberry?"

Chapter 8
Slither Swamp

Doctor Diggitt nodded. "I'll show you," she said. "I brought three bushes from Silver Sea when they were just twigs."

She started toward the end of the garden. "Oh, no!" She sat up on her hind legs and stared.

Pibbin glanced at Leeper. "What's wrong?"

"I can't tell from here," Leeper said. "Must be something about the bushes."

The doctor set off again, and Pibbin hopped close behind her.

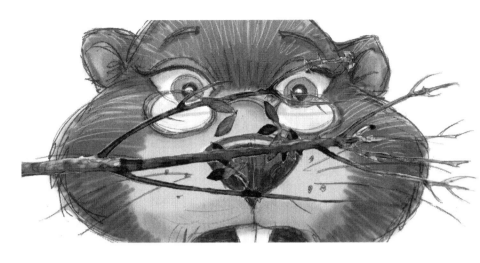

Now he could see the first bush. It had a few tiny green leaves on it.

"Gone!" The doctor growled, low and deep. "Someone's picked off the big leaves."

She looked at the other two bushes and growled again. "I was waiting for them to get ripe, but they're all gone."

"Oh!" Pibbin said. "Couldn't we get a bunch of the small leaves and stick them together?"

"I wish!" Doctor Diggitt pulled off a leaf and held it out to him. "What's that smell like?"

Pibbin sniffed. "Nothing."

Leeper nodded.

"It's not ripe yet," Doctor Diggitt said.

"It has to grow long and thick. Then it starts to smell sweet and gets red spots all over it."

"But something around here smells good," Pibbin said. "Like cookies."

The doctor lifted her nose to the air. "Yes, that's how they smell. The thief probably just finished picking them."

She pointed to the trees beyond the garden. "He must have gone that way, into Slither Swamp. We'll never catch him."

She frowned. "Now, let me think. I can give you some kola root. It might help. And some oil to rub on her foot. And some willow bark, because her leg will hurt for a long time. Poor Sheera!"

Slowly Pibbin said, "Will her leg ever be as good as new?"

The doctor's face drooped. "It might. I have some barberry juice, too. You could try that."

Pibbin didn't want to hear any more. Her words felt like sharp sticks poking into his side.

He looked away from the doctor and tried not to think about Sheera with a leg that would hurt for a long time.

What was that? Something yellow?

He ducked under the fence to see.

A yellow thread. It had caught on the wood of a fence post.

He hopped down the hill, toward the trees at the edge of the bog. Here was a bush with one of those prickly vines hanging from it.

A bit of yellow dangled from the thorns.

"I wonder," he said.

"What?" Leeper said. He was following close behind, and so was the doctor.

Pibbin didn't say any more because the thought scared him. He kept hopping.

"What?" Leeper said again.

"That toad-driver," Pibbin said. "Remember the ties on his boots?"

"Yellow," Leeper said. "You think he's been here?"

"I smelled something sweet on the bus," Pibbin said. "Maybe in the boxes."

Leeper frowned. "Maybe Sweetberry leaves! Maybe he goes around stealing them. Could he sell them down at the shore?"

"He sure could," the doctor said. "Everyone down at the shore wants Sweetberry. Have you seen this thief?"

Pibbin nodded. "He's three times as big as me and really tough."

And he never wanted to see that toad again.

They found another scrap of yellow and started looking for the next.

A mouse ran toward them. "Doctor! Doctor!" she called. "Come quick! Grandpa Mole got a bad cut on his leg."

"I'm sorry," Doctor Diggitt said. "I'll have to go take care of this."

She sighed. "He's heading into Slither Swamp. I don't like to see you going there—too many snakes. I'll catch up as soon as I can."

They hurried through more grass and bushes, and finally reached the swamp. Cedar trees grew all around them, tall and gloomy-green.

No birds sang. No squirrels scampered past. Nothing slithered—not here, anyway.

"Plenty of moss," Pibbin said. "And water."

"And mud." Leeper's big feet made prints in the mud.

"Look," Pibbin said. "Something's been dragged through the moss."

He followed the trail of bent moss stems and kept a watch for slithering things.

The soft black mud felt cool on his feet, and in one muddy patch, he saw faint tracks.

Toad-prints?

Here was a narrow path and another scrap of yellow, snagged by a stump.

Leeper went first, and Pibbin was glad for that. His pal wasn't as wide as the toad, but he was taller.

The trees rose high, and the shadows stretched long—dark enough to hide a toad.

The path twisted and turned past stumps and fallen trees and tufts of grass.

Leeper hopped more and more quickly, and Pibbin tried to keep up.

Ahead of him, Leeper said, "Hey!"

Smack.

Leeper fell.

Pibbin jumped back behind a tree.

He peered out.

The toad-driver held a thick club in his hands. Beside him stood three boxes and a bucket.

In front of him, Leeper lay flat and still.

Chapter 9

Serves You Right

Pibbin held onto the tree with every one of his fingers and toes, and he trembled.

He wanted to climb to the top of the tree and hide.

But . . . Sheera!

He let go of the tree. He grabbed a stick and hopped into the path.

The toad stood there, sturdy as a stump. He saw Pibbin and laughed.

"So, it's my little friend come to visit," he said. "Where's that shiny hoop of yours?"

He stepped forward and swung his club.

Pibbin ducked. He lifted his stick and ran at the toad. His stick hit the toad's boot. It broke.

"Ha!" The toad swung his club again.

Pibbin jumped sideways.

"Wonk!" he yelled. He leaped high—up to the toad's face.

The toad leaned back.

Quick! Try again!

He shot up even higher. He kicked his muddy feet into the toad's eyes.

"Ow!" The toad dropped his club. He covered his eyes. "Ow! Ow!" He fell down and rolled in the moss.

Pibbin snatched up the club and banged it on the toad's head. He grabbed more mud and threw it into his face.

Where was Leeper? Starting to sit up.

Now, what could he do with this toad?

One of the boxes was empty and he tried to move it. Too big.

Leeper pulled himself to his feet. "Good plan. Let me help you."

They leaned on the box and pushed it over the toad so it covered him.

The toad-driver groaned.

Pibbin jumped on top of the box, and so did Leeper.

A horn sounded, far away in the trees. A bike with fat tires rolled closer and closer, making an angry *honk-honk-honk.*

It bounced over the moss and splashed through the mud and stopped beside them.

A little old toad jumped off.

He had a scar on his chin, and he wore blue boots, and he was shouting. "Where'd he go? Where'd he go?"

Fridd.

He stomped his feet. "That kid robbed my friends. He stole my bus. Now he's got it stuck. Have you seen a toad with fancy black boots?"

Pibbin tapped on the box. "In here."

"Let me at him!"

Pibbin and Leeper jumped off the box, and Fridd pushed it over.

The toad-driver sat up, rubbing his eyes. "He kicked me and threw mud at me! I'm going blind."

"Serves you right," the old toad said.

Fridd looked in the bucket, but it was empty, so he opened a box. "More leaves! Where'd you steal them?"

"From my bushes!" A voice growled in the shadows, and Doctor Diggitt hurried toward them.

She reached into the box, and a sweet smell filled the air. "If he picked them too soon, they'll be no good to anybody."

She pulled out a long, thick leaf. It had tiny red spots on it, bright as redbugs.

"Good," she said. "At least they were ripe." She handed the leaf to Pibbin. "Fill up your pack. I'll show you how to make a wrap for Sheera."

She turned back to the toad-driver, lifted him with one claw, and let him dangle.

"I should chop you up for soup."

"No, no!"

"Why did you steal my leaves?"

The toad seemed to shrink, like a balloon gone flat. "I wanted to get rich."

"Fizzle! How foolish!"

She dropped him to the ground in front of his uncle. "Keep him in that box for a couple of days. If he makes a fuss, sprinkle him with red pepper."

"I'll see to it." Fridd looked at Pibbin and Leeper. "Where are you two going?"

"Friendship Bog," Pibbin said. He pushed another handful of leaves into his pack.

"Say hello to Gaffer for me, will you?"

"Okay." Pibbin closed up his pack.

"Looks like you're in a hurry," Fridd said. "You've come this far into the swamp, so keep going west to the Toop River. It'll be faster than going back to the Scar Tree."

Pibbin lifted his pack and slipped it on. Not too heavy. "Okay," he said.

"Just watch out for water snakes," Fridd said. "Some of them have a bad temper."

They thanked the doctor for the leaves, and she told them to thank Sheera for the hoop. Then they set off on the path Fridd had showed them.

"I've heard a lot about water snakes," Pibbin said. "What do they look like?"

"A flat head." Leeper didn't have his usual grin. "Brown with dark bands across the back, like a stick might have. That fooled me once. I almost didn't get away."

"Lots of sticks around here." Pibbin slowed down to check the path as he went.

"You said it. We've got to keep our eyes open."

As they hopped along, Pibbin said, "I've been wondering . . . what's a scar tree?"

"A tree with a scar." Leeper grinned.

Pibbin had to smile. "That's a big help."

"Hmmm. Did you see that scar on Fridd?"

"Kind of like he got hit?" Pibbin said.

"Right. Maybe a scar tree has some sort of mark on it. Where'd you hear about it?"

"Fridd, remember? He said the Toop was faster than going back to the Scar Tree."

Leeper rubbed his head. "I missed that. My head felt like it had flies buzzing inside it."

"You've still got a big bump," Pibbin said. "I thought he killed you."

"So did I," Leeper said. "Thanks for taking care of him, pal."

"You think Fridd's going to give him a dose of red pepper?"

"I hope so!" Leeper glanced up into the trees. "Look at those clouds. Seems like we could touch them if they got any lower. Rain's coming."

Sure enough, rain began to spatter down through the trees, but they didn't mind getting wet. Mist rolled in, cool and thick, until Pibbin could hardly see the bushes beside the path.

He hopped more and more slowly. Where would the snakes be hiding?

The path took a turn, and then another, and another. Were they still going toward the river?

The path curved around a tree, and then all he could see ahead was a wide puddle.

Leeper hopped up beside him. "Hey! What happened to our path?"

The swamp spread around them on every side, with mist as thick as smoke and no sign of a path.

"Where are we?" Pibbin said.

Leeper shrugged. "Don't know."

Pibbin wanted to sit down and rest, but nothing looked safe in this mist. He crawled up onto a stump, and Leeper followed.

"We've got to find a way out of here," Leeper said in a low voice.

Pibbin's pack felt as if it were full of rocks. "Let's look at the map."

Chapter 10
Monster Tree

Pibbin pulled the map out of his pack and unfolded it on the stump.

"Okay," he said. "Here's Wild Bog, and here's Slither Swamp."

"Where's the river?"

"Over here by Slither Swamp."

"The west side, like he said." Leeper sounded worn out. "We should have run into it by now. I wonder if we missed a turn in the path."

"I think so," Pibbin said. He bent over the map. "Look at this mark—it's the same as the one for Gaffer's tree, only bigger."

"Another tree," Leeper said. "Must be a huge one."

"See how it's standing where the swamp ends? I'd like to check around for it."

Leeper sighed. "Might as well try."

Pibbin climbed the nearest tree, all the way to the top. The rain had stopped, but he couldn't see much. He took a careful look at the trees poking through the blanket of mist. One of them seemed especially tall.

Leeper shrugged when he told him. "Lots of tall trees around. Which way is it from here?"

Pibbin waved a hand. "That way. East, right?"

"Yes, that's east," Leeper said. "But we wanted to go west." He closed his eyes, as if his head were hurting again. "Now we don't know anything for sure. See if you can find it."

84

Pibbin took the lead, trying to remember where he'd seen the tree.

He crept through the mist. This one? No. This one? No.

The mist began to thin, and he hurried on. This one? Tall! It seemed to reach all the way to the sky.

He bent backwards and could hardly see the top of it.

He hopped closer, to where the bark had peeled off on one side. The light-colored wood gleamed underneath, looking like a very long and ragged stripe.

"Is that a scar?" he asked.

"Sure is." Leeper stared up at the tree. "What a monster! It probably got hit by lightning."

"Okay," Pibbin said. "If that's the Scar Tree, we're on the edge of the swamp. We can just keep going this way."

"That's right. Friendship Bog is to the north." Leeper rubbed his head again. "I need a nap."

They hopped through a stretch of pine woods. The mist had thinned and the pine needles made a smooth carpet, but Pibbin could hardly drag his feet along. Soon, maybe, they could rest.

After what seemed like a long time, they found themselves at the edge of a small bog.

"Hey, I know this place," Leeper said. He flicked out his tongue for a moth. "We can swim across it, but first, let's take our nap. I'll show you the hollow tree I like to use."

They slept for the rest of the day, feasted on water bugs, and started their swim by the light of the stars. Before the sun rose, they had crossed the bog and reached a stream with ferns growing along its banks.

"This is Singing Stream!" Pibbin said. "It comes out of Friendship Bog." He hopped faster and faster. Soon they'd be home!

At the top of the stream, they crossed the old beaver dam and turned to follow the shore. They hurried past some yellow water lilies, and Ticklegrass Field, and Woodpecker Log.

Was Sheera still alive? Was Corey taking good care of her? What about her leg?

At last they reached Sheera's pool.

Corey jumped up. "Hurrah!"

Sheera turned her head. Her leg looked stiff, and it had a crust of dried blood on it, but her eyes glowed.

"So glad to see you," she whispered.

Pibbin pulled a handful of leaves out of his pack. He made a thick wrap for her leg, the way the doctor had showed him.

"Oh!" Sheera said. "Oh, yes!"

Corey smiled. "How does it feel?"

"Warm," Sheera said. "Like when I'm sleeping in the sun."

Corey turned to Pibbin. "You did it!" he said. "I wish I'd gone. I wish . . ."

He looked down at his toes, and Pibbin knew what he was thinking.

"Don't feel so small," he said. "You took care of Sheera, and your map took care of us."

He leaned close to the little striped frog. "You've got a big heart. That's what counts."

Corey looked up. "Did you happen to see the Scar Tree? I put a tall tree on my map because an old squirrel told me it was there."

"We sure did, thanks to your map," Leeper said. "It's not very far from the hill where Doctor Diggitt lives. We didn't know that when we were wandering around in the swamp."

"Diggitt's Hill!" Corey said. "Show me where, and I'll mark it on my map."

Carpenter dived off a lily pad to join them, and Bug-Master hopped through the bushes.

"We heard a news flash from the peepers," Carpenter said. "You found some Sweetberry!"

Leeper told them the whole long story, and Pibbin watched Sheera smile. He felt as warm as sunlight, too.

"Aha!" Carpenter said. "A thief! That's why no one around here could get Sweetberry leaves. Old Gaff will be glad to hear this."

He nodded to Pibbin. "Good to see you made it back okay."

"Great work, both of you," Bug-Master said in his ringing voice. "I'm proud of you, small Pibbin. You're growing up fast."

"Fast, fast, fast!" sang the peepers.

Pibbin looked at Leeper and grinned. "Thanks, pal!"

end
of
Tale 1

Map of Friendship Bog

From Book 2 : *The Story Shell*

They had to find a place to hide.

Books by Tim Davis

Tim is a longtime illustrator for *Highlights* magazine, specializing in Hidden Pictures.

He has also illustrated several books, including the following titles:
The Cranky Blue Crab
Pocket Change
Once in Blueberry Dell

The Friendship Bog Series:
Pibbin the Small
The Story Shell

Books written and illustrated by Tim Davis

Mice of the Herring Bone
Mice of the Nine Lives
Mice of the Seven Seas
Mice of the Westing Wind, Book One
Mice of the Westing Wind, Book Two
Tales from Dust River Gulch
More Tales from Dust River Gulch

Visit Tim's website at
http://www.timdaviscreations.com

Books by Gloria Repp

For ages 2-8
Noodle Soup
A Question of Yams

The Friendship Bog Series:
Pibbin the Small *
The Story Shell *

For ages 9-12
The Secret of the Golden Cowrie
The Mystery of the Indian Carvings *
Trouble at Silver Pines Inn

Adventures of an Arctic Missionary Series:
Mik-shrok
Charlie
77 Zebra

For ages 12 and up
The Stolen Years
Night Flight
Nothing Daunted *

*available in digital format

Visit Gloria at http://www.gloriarepp.com
for story resources and discussion questions.

Made in the USA
Charleston, SC
03 October 2012